Acknowledgments

Special thanks to Lyndsey Sickler for graciously letting me use an edited version of one of their pictures for the cover of this project.

Introduction

Don't Touch Me is an exploration…. "What does Love mean?" and "How do you define it?" Even though I believe that my answers to these questions will never be complete. I now know through working on this collection that Love is sometimes dark and sometimes conflicting. That Love is personal and tangled up in what we *actually* feel and; what we are *told* we should feel. Some of the poems in this collection are raw and seductive while others are standoffish and coy. Some are expressions of angst and sadness while others wear angst lightly and if you scratch the surface are actually shy representations of fragile hope and wonder. Thank you for taking the time to follow my attempt to give these poems a voice and a life.

CW: Some of the poems in this collection contain adult themes

Don't Touch Me

Mostly I am
made from tissue thin fragile moments
delicately when I was so dangerously brazen
watching you sleep
too patient too
open too vulnerable and
It hurts too much
to say I trust myself
to trust you
It never lasts anyways and always
the causal beginning brush of fingertips
scatters me to pieces and again everything changes and again
everything
becomes somewhat less than and more
commonly placed
mundane but I want
to believe the lies my body
tells me I want to believe in
warm velvet skin
supple arms
and broad shoulders
I want to believe there is more than finding myself
awake
tangled in my body
open and vulnerable
fragile
delicate telling myself to savor
this perfect moment

Only The Body

Thirty-Eight years spent
mindlessly mouthing
      the same
      sour
      flesh
hollowed chest packing a six-chambered heart.
      And they say its ok--
      take the safety off-
      And They tell me someday
someday soon
but still I am always right here cutting teeth
my own
raised-dead
flesh.
Thirty-Eight years-
      chewing through
      lips, cheeks, and tongue
and everyone tells me be patient
hold still—breathe
wait
but I need this to mean something more than
      the same tired lines the same
      dead flesh
but I need to feel something
more than
the empty
screaming violence
They left me with.

In Relation

I am almost used to it now-
 just another ordinary day full of
empty nothing
thoughts and I have
too often make due with
bits of bone and other forgotten forms of currency. And I have too often
made myself of smooth surfaces
and brittle skin
adorning myself in twists of hair and chipped-toothed
smiles but
I get it now.
there was never anything here for you
all the parts of me I tried to give you-

bits of bone, knots of hair, and empty shells
barely made it to face value.

Armistice

You have your weapons
warm lips and breath so
soft so insistently demanding
your fingers move celebrating
my secret bends and curves and each and every
scar
I tried so innocently to
hide.
Your eyes reflective
hesitantly hopeful
and expectant and I
gave you everything I held inside me
every guilty pleasure
and semi-shamefully- sacred
desire
I surrendered my body
crouched low like a supplicant
curled inside hollow
worn stones
at your feet.

Honest Monster

I always had a tendency to hide myself in silences and the
passing sounds of other people's conversations
trying to convince myself you couldn't mean it
when you would say that you were nothing
without me building myself from
every time
I sat sleepless watching the sun force its way
into my insecurities and
weak longing like a testament of
how I couldn't live
without you. And it is true...
we loved to
play our games--
you pushing your way into anyone
that would have you and I
pretending nothing
you could ever do
would ever hurt me.
Such a perfect makeshift monster—

we thought we were everything we thought
we had left to hold on to.
And somehow you thought I was
the only one you thought would ever
forgive you.

Solomon

Back before
hidden in the corners of
                    cushions-- in basements
you dealt with me
fairly, desperately, and
relentlessly
you gave me
the curves and planes of my own body
shaping me out of hushed whispers and the callouses of your hands
you
                    slid over me-- increasing me
with each red flushed crested wave and
the sun barely saw us
through the languid movements of small glass eyes
above our bodies twisted into a sweat-stained
languages we barely had the air to speak.

And I remember I was so light
and you pressed down anchoring me with your weight
reaching up to cup my cheek and you held
so me tight as if with joyous surrender you sought to defy
                    the movements of heaven.

Back then I believed everything you every told me and
I could taste the crispness of your lips and you gave me
the seeds of your body
like salt whenever I would lick my lips.

And This Is What I Have:

A cinder block heart
stretching sinew
streams, rivers, and the secret
breath of oceans under
thick and lazy
skin.
dust-filmed empty rooms
hallways and sour metal
sweat slicked gravity
broken teeth and bleeding
gums
patched worked in ink and
swollen scars
crumbled paper hearts and the
dreams of poems
and nothing
for no one for
very long.

Pine

green needles down
the lingering scent-
sharp; distinct
>and I can still remember the way I would
>roll you between my fingers
>so much of you being- so much a part
>from me.

I am starting to believe that
I am like winter and
I am starting to believe that
I can finally catch my breath...
Back before that day you said you wanted to plant flowers in my
chest unconcerned with
the way I twisted and crawled-
>always reaching
>desperate for you and
>you were the center

of my everything.
And how you would smile and laugh at the ways my body would
bend.
Desperate and always reaching
outward and I never asked--
How you felt that last day with me standing
outside while you shut me inside myself
Did it feel like a job well done?
And you moved casually crushing brittle stems and leaves; petals
beneath your feet.
>so sharp as if to pierce my skin.
>leaving me to curl myself slow
>and causally downward stunted fingers
>half reaching

encasing myself in dirt and pocket lint and tiny bits
of brittle leaves and stems.
Finally
I am starting to believe I am growing

into something that could be
      so much a part from you and much more
      like myself
      I am starting to believe
      I am my own connections
unfolding slowly with thin green needle heart beats
down; lingering and distinct.
Finally.
I am starting to believe I can breathe again.

A Pale Substitute

But I tried to give you
everything my
love--
there was just so many things
I didn't know how to feel.
And so I muddled through with apologies.
half-hearted but
not quite I
only had the shadows of shapes but rarely did I have
the substance.
In my way I am still constantly seeking ways to honor you
my love, I should have done better but
I am pale clay and pitted flesh
crudely made
dirt and ash I never had
sunlight for very long and I would
offer you desperate
fire and sacrifice and would offer you
fragile love and scarred flesh
crudely made with dirt and ash
I never held sunlight quite long enough
My love I only felt
its paler substitute

Telling the Hours

Could love be ?
the slow tearing of skin
patient detachment
bruised bones
and crashing waves
slowly
      moving cycles-
      angles and edges
      grit, endurance,
      and the
      never ending
      need
      for deeper waters.

Mixed Metaphors and Innuendo

You always were more than cold enough
a distant galaxy
spinning further and further
away
empty and vast
constantly pulling
everything inside your ever expanding
influence.
You always were greedy
a dry socket
aching for all the things you wish I was
you always were so kind
complacently crafting
me in rounder edges
to define the place
you said I fit
inside you.

Not What We Did but What We Do

There should be room enough here
when everything we do in tenderness
comes to roost in notched curves in
bones
and the fire's carefully banked.
At one time at once delicate
and indulgently sensual loosing ourselves in
ridges and grooves we
trace hands draping
   the raiment of skin we
   dance our souls a
   mummer's dance
of corners and the
supple sway of hands
and we pivot wrist and elbow
making each embrace
   a show of columns and lines and
   all the ways we allow ourselves
   happiness.

Paperweight

Quick
but fading by degrees
almost measurable in
finer lines
the way you always
looked expectant
not giving me
anything but smooth marble
only if my shoulders could bear
your histories
your stories your
weight
quickly fading we
moved like clouds
pretending we are more than
air displaced and hope
we loved
like a razor's edge
finer lines and
the way I tried to pin you down
if only my shoulders could bear the weight
histories mean nothing stories mean
nothing when I can barely feel you
when you give me
nothing but the grinding
of smooth marble.

For Kevin

(retroactively)

I moved too quickly
then
trying to prove I could kindle
fire
from dust and ashes
blind corners and
empty rooms. Because
you were like sunlight to me
lazy like a summer evening
and just as benevolent. And
I thought I could hide myself
inside you and
I thought I was so worldly
so cryptic and wise
But I am no phoenix
racing the horizon with orange and red wings ringing in glory
I am land-locked I am foolish
fragments disjointed advances and
awkward pauses
not enough give your life
to burn you down.

All the Ways I Can't

Slowly surrounded
threads of skin
somewhat thinning in places
where I am left
to place my feet
every second and every day
the same.
        I tell you-
        I breathe for you
        selfish in the ways I want
        you and I can't even pretend
        you exist.
All the words I was ever given
muscles and tendons
threads of skin
arch and curve and
Every second of every day
grooves of every day actions repeated
selfishly I breathe for you
        another lie I tell myself
        you exist
        and I can't even pretend.

One Kind of Prayer

Not quite like pain
but there is
as much of a sharpness as
a sweetness
       fierce like defiance
to grasp and tear the sameness of walls that surround
us that surround
Heaven.
Not quite like despair
but there is as much of helplessness as
there is resourcefulness
       devoted like a promise
willing to surrender
my very breath itself.
       Remember this
no matter what no matter
the distance or
where life takes us
       you will never be alone
       for I will be with you
       defiantly devoted
until and over
the very walls of heaven.
       I promise.

Love Songs For Ghosts

My love could be a partly truth so much
more intense
like mourning
like that slow inevitable descent
so close we could almost be
so painfully entwined
and I make
temporary companions with the silence
around me
clenching my teeth to suffer
the distance to travel between
dusk and dawn.
It could be mostly what we have left
of truth
and my head is full of flittering ghosts fanning outward
like fingers and the memories we
probably once called passion
and I am so aware of
the limits of my skin
we were so close
almost-but-not-quite
I once thought I could wish
for more.

Anchor

Every memory is clear
razor edged and
I wish I could hate you
with thin sliced skin stained with alcohol peeling and
curling into tobacco-stained
warmth
and everything I used to know
the grit of your hands and your smothered musk
of salt
and
we might have had the weight of oceans
the stinging press of air
and I wish I could
hate the memory of every sure languid movement
of your body and the way you
made me believe
I was safe
secure
weighted down
drowning
in the curved pressing weight of your arms.

A Quarter Gone

I am made of
absences
well-intentioned
missed chances
hollow spaces
match-sticks
thick ugly scars
and incomplete stitching.
I am made of
bones
slightly off-center
corners
blinded slick bricks
crumbling foundations
carrying quite a bit of extra baggage
wrapped in tangled rope tongue.
I am made of bruised blues and purples
swollen knuckles
busted lips
blisters and burns
rusted nails
see through
plastic skin and such a sweet
sugar candy smile.

For Love

You were the blade
well-oiled iron your body a slender
keen edge
and I didn't care
my body was already covered
with thick lines and scars
puckering and pulling at my skin.
You were an
open flame
insatiable with a sweat wet
fevered touch
and I didn't know
my body was made from silent
awkward motions
and puppet strings.
You were an
well-worn affliction
tearing me apart
with sharp sticky fingers
leaving swollen blisters in the passage of your fingertips
and I didn't care
because I was able to pretend you
needed me
 if only as a willing victim.

Stunt Double

It would be easier if I could
borrow other words like
broken bits of plastic and
glass
tinkling and sweet to the ear
It would be easier if I
had the perfect stand-in
my body would be
exacting
to your
desires for dimensions
and I would just fit
like in the movies a
make-believe ugly duckling
hidden behind thick glasses but
I am only as much as
I can be caught in a frozen frame
and nowhere near
happily-ever-after

Figment Of A Melancholy Oscillating Picture Box.

I will be that ghost silently tucked along the edges
a random pattern of light and shadows occasionally sliding across
the wall a
pocket-sized collection of odds and endings
a camera box mind of subjective lens and rose colored filters
fitted to a passing whisper that sometimes doubles
as breathy vowels and a conspiracy of consonants
that rarely travels past your lips.
I will be that mute memory spinning through
hastily captured moments pressed flush against the film
a projection of random stops unraveled in a half-heard
story that nags at you with a tip-of-the-tongue familiarity
until maybe you see me moving just a bit removed
a guilty pleasure or maybe an
inside joke remember so many years after the fact and
you might realize that because of you
 and this moment
I exist.

Lure

Free fall
phone calls
the bottom drops out
the dead waits
hooked fingers pulling
at your mouth.

Quick sand

demands

eventually

ghosts move

taking breath

in subtle motions

of teeth

tongue

lips

whispers with tiny
pulling at your
mouth

Ready-Made.

After all you
came to me in pieces
plaster casted heart
prepackaged

some assembly
required.

and I could pretend
a cardboard cutout kind of love
fully pose-able
or double your money back.

limited edition- act
now while supplies
last.

and I could pretend
you could be
everything
pressing my lips to the divots of your skin
you could be everything I
lack.

double your money back some assembly
required

act now operators are standing by
prepackaged sold
separately

and you don't feel
but I can pretend
I loved you after all

you came to me.

I Decided to Tell

I feel this
often in echoes my lead plated heart like
the strings are
cut.
And in their place is a hollow and crushing
wait
the world sinks
downward and inward
too quickly collapsing and
it
takes
too
long
to catch my breath and you
forget you are still here
gasping desperate in the frantic
scrambling and tearing for air and you are
useless you fold inward pivoting at your lungs and waist collapsing
to your knees
you give in
to the relentless gravity of heartbreak
and nothing
else matters and nothing else makes sense again.

Tuesday at 3pm We'll Have Coffee…

Just pretend that you never heard this before
a too classic tale of two people curled up with a coffee table
between them
bright glass windows, picture frames and pop culture.

Everything fits
and it is almost too easy

We can choose to believe with a kind of studied casualness that is
all
so important these days and each publically well-known
private word is so carefully scripted

copied from advice columns, movie screens, the sage suggestions of
a talking head
on the radio
everything just fits
two people so intimately displayed leaning closer lips almost
touching

and they know it is just pretend but it is almost too easy
digging dirty nails into each other's paper thin skin
lips stained and bleeding gums
so much dumb meat
everything is so bright
glass windows, picture frames, two people curled at a coffee table
a classic tale every one pretends they never heard before.

The Dead Have No Dreams

Tonight, I will hang corpse candles to
drape the sky's bones in
patterns of memories and lace patterned
in pale grey, silver white, and a smooth
velvet sable brown.
I will cradle each glowing pale yellow spark
clasping my hands under and around my
own ghost
slightly hesitant vulnerable
in love
hollow bones
echoed eyes
harder heart.
Tonight, I will kill the body; breaking each joint and angle
boiling it down with half-heard prayers and mis-placed hope
leaving behind
 only dust and tallow a charming little conceit for a broken heart
a silly little secret whispered to the wind
I will let myself drift and cling to dark tree limbs and the undersides
of shadows
like brief blaze birthing cigarette smoke
 before
feathered soft in owl's wings I pull myself past your body's warmth
and lose myself to
the horizon.

Reversible Armor

Hey, it's just another
5am slow fall
Sunday morning T.V.
muted glow
flickering glimpses
of off-white walls
a relationship of snapshots the memories of your scent
curling around me and
I'm barely moving excess flesh
mal-formed yet somehow find myself racing full tilt
slightly off-center in repressed
razor blade thoughts I find myself
worn smooth with frayed edges
pitted in places re-tread
circular motions a tightrope stumbling gravity
inward with tighter orbits
closed circuit
disconnect damages reversible armor razor cuts thin lines tight rope
sleep walk T.V.
muted barley moving mal-formed Sunday morning smooth frayed
edges re-tread
endlessly flickering off-
white walls stumbling in smaller tighter orbits closed circuit
snapshot
relationships of excess flesh pitted in places 5am slow fall
don't blink.

You Walked Me Home

Tonight the streetlights
buzz and mutter reaching outward
hazy glow and your arm is
a comfortable reminder
warm across my shoulders and
I am tucked like a puzzle piece
in the spaces you give me.
We move in our own kind of rhythm
pacing the length of our shadows
planning our lives heads slightly bent
like conspirators we share our secrets
in low whispers and bright laughter
while the streetlights
buzz and
mutter
you walk beside me
fitted like puzzle pieces
completely connected
and where ever you are and as
long as I am with you
I know
I am safe.

Subtle Motions Of Lips And Tongue

And this is true you
gave the secrets of my body
straining sinew and crashing
waves.
And I felt like I fit
rolling you between my fingers
a pale substitute for the need
for gravity.
And you were indulgently
sensual draped in a raiment
of sweat and warm velvet
skin.
I would breathe for you
a lit cigarette
to catch my breath
you gave me
blind corners and empty rooms
and my body
a love song left for ghosts and memories.

A.N.S.A

You are to me combined in memories of rain slick
pavement painted
roadsides of grey, black, and
white I think of
Cheap shoes and
midnight shifts.
When I think of you I think of
collecting myself outside at your door step
making another choice
after hours of greasy spoons
steam
dishpan hands and
chipped nails to let myself in and I
think of how you don't really care about what brought me once
again
standing hesitant under a dimly lit porchlight just
as long as you can taste my skin and
bite my lips and
tell me how good it feels and
I wonder if it is even
worth it.

It was me.

When you are out there sometimes-
too long.
I can't see what part of your shadow is
you or me.
And we said today was not enough if all is left
to be alone-
to be alone.
And you said
        "It should be...darker...somehow"
pulling yourself from the windows edge slightly
haunted by the phantoms that you could not help but
leave-
still. And I
believed everything and every word you said caught up
across a rough-hewn room indrawn hugging my knees
amidst pillows and cigarette smoke not
daring in my silence not wanting to curl my lips
around the same too tired lies-
        But sometimes
when you are gone too long I am left to feel the shadows of what
we were before everything went
wrong.

Your Ghost Deconstructed

These days I
can almost hear you breathing
benedictions in the phantoms you left
even now
long after the rush of words became
barely remembered you left me impressions faint
tones of bodies enmeshed in the movements of bones, tendons,
pain and ever present need
for heat

I can almost see you through
buzzing vibrations sliding past conscious thought and
memory and I wonder about the lives we
could have lived before

where I would wake up beside you
too afraid to smooth away your slept-in sweat damp almost-too-
long
bangs for fear of waking you. And somehow that seems more real
to me than
these days with only your ghost to keep me
safe.

2 A.M.

I might be,
silently becoming
no one
slowly fading the edges
of you and what we had
blurring the distinction
between have and need.
I might be,
the one that stands watching dark become
colder
 misting the glass with
should's and maybe's
blurring difference with my breath.
I might be,
awestruck and mute hugging myself hoping to
keep the boundaries safe- to keep all the desperate razor blade
desires

inside a make-believe martyr to keep you safe and in this moment

I might be anyone

surging towards the horizon.

Am I Cassandra?

I never knew
nobody could tell me and maybe he actually did
mean it but sunlight was
his weapon
and he was
tan and young with smooth
confident skin he was blonde, blue eyed,
a compassionate
colonist
so sure his feet rarely touched the
ground he graciously kept my heart in a
discount tin one more of a multitude and
I never saw all the times he took my
broken flesh, stone and clay lifting himself higher
sunlight was his weapon and
nobody could tell me
no one could ever be more honest and no one
would ever be more true
and no one would listen
he would never be as cruel
as I was
and nobody would tell me
the exact moment I forgot how much it meant
to dream

Life and Times of Pantry Boy

It was harder then
growing up on a desert island where
the body I was in was not
allowed to want the body
I was in.

Back then
it was better to be frivolous
cheap plastic and cellophane watching
imaginary lives flicker on the t.v. screen
than to taste myself in
another
busted bloody
lip

      because everyone knows
      boys will be
      boys as long
      as they will be boys

It was harder then
the gravel tore at my knees with jagged stone and the
memories
of coal crossed with yellow tape and
no matter how I closed my eyes I could
not quite convince myself
that
a handful of stolen moments when no one
was watching was
anything close to sweeten the bitter taste of grit and ash
 because everybody knows that
the body I was in was not allowed...

Not Quite Dirt

You were standing
in the back row
a single silhouette
a flame flirting
backlit in the glare of everything I knew I was not allowed
to be and I placed you inside me; cradled you like the

violence of every
bite-sized production of every commercially consumed
colored
pixel meant
nothing you shattered yourself in the excess another fell in
dying trails of fireflies
at your feet.

I watched you sliding your eyes
around the grooves
a glancing blow relegating everything else
to the background and I

      wondered what roles were left to me
      after last lingering glow of you
      was gone.

Post-Modern Elegy

We make up stories
gathering bits of second-hand romance or whatever
 catches our eyes
creating whole-cloth personalities to
fool ourselves
into thinking it's all part of some great
narrative we tell
ourselves it is more
it has to be
more than flotsam. And I

like to pretend the same
like I knew you for years the same
building walls...this is me and
this is you making stories of
gathered bits of romance
that caught my eye
a fool for comfort

of a person I never knew.

Downward Goes the Iron Queen

More by the lack then
by happenstance
we came to justify the seasons
even when the body is way past dead we
try to give meaning to its progression

and iron cage heart filled with petals bruised

lazily summer shifts into bright mourning
winter is coming the body remembers

Downward goes the Iron Queen crowned in marigolds and
oleander

just lay back and relax and eventually
one day you will come to enjoy it.

Doll

No
do not look at me.
I can see
only

mud, earth, darkness and
the time spend and the distance.

and this feels like nothing feels like
business as usual and I can not
be anything
unless it hurts I want to move I
want to move I want to
stop
it only drags on and my failures mean

nothing means
business as usual.

no
do not look at me I
wear my scars too proudly I wear
my history in the downward curve of my
face and the lilt of my voice I am
darkness and moist earth I am
dirt I want to move I want to move I
want
more than these walls around me not
reaching out
careful I am afraid
of what you could want to
expect I feel like nothing and I can not

believe I can see

bits and pieces patchwork beauty and I
want to be all the things
you say you
see in me
but
I am not.

So; People Build Levees

push past
bleached white bones
of riverbeds chocked tangled grass and
dry cracked mud
and maybe

      if my voice was a siren's song
      if held a nightingale-thrush I
would sing to you I would
lead you past
bleached white bones and chocked river beds and
my words
      would
      fill you with anything other than
      the memory of barely healed scars and
      overgrowth.

Soliloquy

Sometimes, it is true, I think of
separations and
all the things I never told you

my lips never pressed to the curving of thin bones
and even thinner flesh and

I barely speak of dreams
anymore unless
the lights are low holding only echoes I
hide myself in a whisper I

just wanted to be enough for once....I just wanted
to be enough and

Sometimes, it is true, I think of all the reasons and
ways I break myself against these unsaid
conversations

And no I am not what we thought I was anymore I
shed myself in the ever changing stream of you
just-happening-to-pass-by.

Sometimes, it is true I hide myself in a whisper
in the movement of lips barely moving

I am still trying....why....am I still trying?

For Shadows

Dawn and I are
in between
waiting you said I
carried sunshine once and
maybe I closed my eyes
and turned my head but
for one second I believed
in inevitable gradual
shifts when
the world gets brighter and
you said
I closed my eyes and
turned my head too
afraid of what was in front of
me.

After The Apocalypse

You say, our love is delicate,
like ash floating in the breeze. You say
our love is like a fire — it burns brighter as it consumes.
And we are two people dancing in the sun.
And you say
If thunder rolls our love is desperate
a craving to wet our lips.

    our love is bold, for being so bright and fleeting
    ash like grey petals swirling to our feet.
    paper thin and delicate
    a craving to wet our lips.

A Like Comparison

So like love he
was open space he
didn't exist he
lived in two-dimensions he was
empty hands
missed chances
stone walls
unreadable
inscrutable he was
a dumb muscle beating a
body made from
broken promises
and pleasant lies so
like love he
didn't exist.

Spun Glass

I love your lips
your teeth
the velvet of your
skin
your
dense solid weight
I love
your hips
the way your elbow bends
the meat of your
thighs
your scent
musky and sweet
primal and
intoxicating
a private space
you let me
in

Scene Queen

Mostly though I am it seems
I am out-of-fashion
gathering dust in a shoebox heart
       years passing in an accumulation of
       sixty-second snapshots. I button up on
       the left my bones full of cement and I
       am too tired to change- And everybody still
       wants the tall, dark, man well defined
       with pre-fabricated edges. And I am

made up
a few awkward encounters and more
       than my share of empty space
       Decades too late

and growing older in
sixty-second
increments.

Fine Print.

After all you
came to me in pieces a
plaster-casted heart
pre-packed

     some assembly required.

and I could close my eyes and
pretend a
cardboard cutout kind of love
fully poseable
or double your money back

     limited edition
     act now while supplies last.

and you could be everything
and you could be everything
I could never believe I could be
double your money back some assembly required
pre-packaged may not be available in all states and

     I don't feel but
     I pretend
     I love you but
     you don't.

First In Shadow, Then In Light

Today, I thought I saw you
casting shadows
across the horizon and I
quickly turned my head
so I wouldn't have to see

and I once again swallowed my
voice now a whisper when
once it was a scream and I
filled my chest with iron bars
and I filled my chest with a
rusted heart and

still the dead can never tell.

I know
I lost you everyday
I know
your voice
more like a memory
than a dream and you are
so full of light
in those moments
standing separate
from the sky

that loves you like I do
quietly sliding my body
into the shadows you left
behind
forgotten and
useless
since the dead can never tell.

An Almost Swansong

And here we find ourselves finally
tracing the lines
the inconsistancies
no really
it has come to this
a distance of what you say and
that look on your face
from time to time

> When you wanted more than what we could have been
> more than just us
> together and

all the times I thought we were content because
I was and
you let me play
the part and maybe
we were
just two people content

> to act it out like we knew
> it was scripted and we
> didn't want to be alone

But in between baiting breaths and
stage dark quiet

we knew .

Bits Of String

Maybe, I say
if I had more time I would
nurture these fraying cords
adding
knots and bits of shiny
colored glass
smooth river washed bones
and late autumn afternoons
spend playing in the river's bed.
I want
to say that there will be time
to follow each braided line back
before
when I knew for sure why
I hold so tightly to
this things
that never
were.

Some Days Like Fire

It is true we might never know the depth
lost as we are mostly lost among fragments of story and
myth-
never questioning the telling ways our
bodies dance in shadows along the walls.

We constantly thread our fragile fires around artifice
into
and through
concrete, mud, shells,
pavement, and bones.

Ultimately,
there are no answers here
only the shapes your lips make and the play
our hungers lying
deep like a lonely ache
we name desire and
fear.

Maybe, we might say
it is better that we scatter ourselves more thinly
into lifetimes lived in the tiniest of movements and a
parade of painted pretty little lies
that we wrap in garish make-believe
promises.

Pulling flesh tight and
tighter still around broken
bricks, bones, and
sinew
our eyes constantly tracking the telling ways
we slide our skin
reaching

empty we consume we

only get these hints of the things we told ourselves we never could
forget
the spaces and textures we thought we knew of what we should
have been
huddling closer in whispers of dying light we tell ourselves we
remember
the lives we lived
the hunger of crashing flames and
what we still owe.

Ex-Machina

Broken down
it is only slightly more than
tendons
    bones
pulling skin

the furnace burns in a cage of
gilded metal twisted
thorns and

      the need for breath

an empty space cooling
inside me
a measured sense of missed chances and
passers-by

each palm has its own textures
its own way of asking

      slightly more than
      tendons
        bones
      pulling skin

Broken down
into empty spaces
cooling gilded cages
of metal and thorns
missed chances
and the need
for asking
the comfort of gravity
pulling us closer.

Please. Wait.

We had
mostly a relationship made echoes and
 of footsteps

conversations built out of cigarette smoke
and for days at a time I
would pull you over my shoulders
marveling at the way the muscles of
your body
made me feel safe.

      We had
      a love made from steel wool
      gauged by how far my neck
      could bend and
      I marveled at the soft harshness
      your lips and your words
      giving me shape

We had
fire burning need
      and I marveled at how the muscles of your body
made me happy
to suffer.

Eos

And this is grey
soothing indecision
comfortable
silence a
slow movement
tracing her curves
the warmth of her
breath
she
holds this moment perfect
in the folds of her skin
and underneath

the tension of coiled muscle a
slight pause a rocking movement
bending she mimics the horizon
calming rising
she rests on palms and the balls of bare feet
pressing down
coiled muscle and perfect skin
the sweat gathers at her lips
and the way she tastes

her body shapes shadows into
a rainbow of possiblities
and you can feel your heart
quickening
the dryness of your need
you inhale her scent
her confident freedom

she finds her release springing forward
in a blur of angles and curves a body
born for movement and

before you can think to call her name
she leaves you behind.

Anniversary 2010

Since
it is all that i
have I will
love her bones
and the earth above
I will love the reflective
surface of the stone he gave her and

the strangeness of seeing her vacant
in photographs.

I will love
the slow dull ache
she left behind her

I will coat my body in dust
and ashes giving her salt
and the dryness of my lips I
will adorn myself in
the stories I remember
and in memories I
can trust I
will stumble barefoot
through paved lines of city streets through
gravel roads

Goblin

You never missed an opportunity to tell me
I was such strange fruit
browning on the vine
but the earth is rich
breathing secrets
       your skin is thin each vein is desperate
       lips pull and tug
       and youth has given you teeth sharp enough
weight is ponderous and soft
fur from the outside
in
each seed believes what it is told
       your arms are so thin you never
       get your fill and your lips
       pull and tug
       and youth has given you teeth and
 scar tissue
and every can see
curling leaves starving
thin tendrils of soft rot
a bladed tongue you
break the skin wet your lips
with pulsing veins
but the earth is rich
breathing secrets and one day
you too will be
adored.

Memento Diligo

Of course I don't know what I need
lately all I see is
bones moving
muscles under
skin
        a cold hearth made from worn stone
            a collection of smothering soot somewhat
swirling grey clouds quickly subdued
my heart.
Each facet weathered burnt
fingers probing smooth reflective surfaces

I don't feel this
mostly
I keep moving
        picking up an assortment of awkward
            apparatuses and make-do meanings and
the words I guess I am supposed to say the problem
is me
rusted gears
grinding clockwork
building tension and
nothing.
Of course I don't know what I need
        I am barely keeping warm with what I allow
            myself to feel.

Survivor's Guilt

We are barely holding on

Old histories of random encounters

the tangle of barely covered arms.

Wistfully lost in the moment

All sails lead clear

we shudder bodies becoming

desperately hopeful

with no land in sight we

only to take a smaller death

Someone For Everyone

Love, you almost made it
you
  followed at a slower pace I already had my scars in place
                        my veins thinner under a thick skin
nothing of mine remembers nothing
more tender
and I might of given you
rose petals
and whatever secrets were left
my body and I might have
submerged myself
feeling my warm slide along
like clouds collected
so soft
lazy patterns left in the wake of
                    iron and other crimson metals
                            and
                everything I could leave you
                        my body
my love can only carry
me
so far.

A Typical Love Song

Abrasive underneath
coils of gold amber and strips of flesh
burrow down packed earth
        we hide warmth in sacrifice in
the spaces our bones leave us
    we are not quite windows and in-between
eyes
vitreous humors we
            glut ourselves in a harvest of grain and promises
we know now
we will never keep.
bodies can only take so much bodies
worn thin
hold tight to each stinging blade
stalk and root
each breath a shallow pantomime
lessons learned under the cool glare
of Thursday night sitcoms
what is and
what will always be fine grit matchmaking we
      hide fire in packed earth
and the spaces our bones left us
coils
of flesh open arms
      so many shallow embraces we
only know what we have been told we are
allowed
and the secrets we hoard in what bodies we
can keep safe can keep
hidden.

Reckoning

If when you say I am
made up
        artificial
the heart is constant
         even as the meaning changes
We always seem to find ourselves in
 dirt
wax
       flaking skin and random moments of circuitry
the re-invention of the sounds our bodies can make

and there is nothing left to forgive it seems

the heart pushes us erratically into half-forgotten
         corners but you say there is
room enough to fit comfortably inside

conveniently forgetting past negotiations of bones
ligaments
        worn down muscles and the
heart remains
          as you say
          artificial.

The Painful Bruising Truth

At one time I fell in love in
your absence and I
believed
        paper airplane letters coded inside
        random song lyrics, safety pins and
all the ways I painted myself in

I tried

        giving you my breath mouthing
        greeting card meanings desperately hoping
to keep myself almost hidden

I tried giving you the slow motion creaks and whispers
of yawning tree limbs and impossible
situations where I made sense and you would know
but
    nothing fit the way I thought I felt so you
never knew
that time I almost said
you were
everything to me.

A Cutting Glance

This ghost shivers the
most; when you are around but
all you see is skin.

Clockmaker

Small deaths and tiny hands
move in waves
      holding only the slightest hesitation and
we always said
                we could find our way back
frequent faces in between
                  the way you taste.
Little lies and tiny hands
eventually everything looks the same
                bodies move with burning breath
and everything seems so urgent we
always said we find
              our way back
eventually.

I Am Just Catching My Breath

It's possible I
whisper just so
I can feel the shapes my words would make
if I had the courage maybe
I close my eyes
straining my hears
hoping to catch the softly sharp
intake of breath whenever
you turn away never showing you
loneliness
contains
Its own
forms of gravity
making the spaces left in everyday moments more
expansive and
somehow a lifetime becomes somehow
more
significant

Tin Man's Lament

Oh, it is much too late

you see I

only carry dull flickers in my rusted nickel-plated

chest

and I only now can see my bones are

thin and stagnant and

clamors with empty space and I

can't

I am sorry you say

     you are falling in love-

          I didn't mean it.

Ugly Duckling

Shh...
 remember to count your steps the
tissues of our bodies are
not any kind of
roadmap and the way we feel
tracing curves against our skin
waiting for the lights to change
and
we could live here in
this space here
unfinished and ugly
remember
the ways our bodies move downward
is just another kind of love and
we could live
in sour breath and bloody noses
perfect
never taking another step.

I Will Always

Who will I become without you?
all my mistakes and
everything I let myself lean on
                              the earth never really pulls you in
it is just blood
sinking beneath your skin so
let's just say I would just
let myself—but
everywhere outside is cruelly smooth and I
carry your casket barely breathing
braced in swollen scar tissues inside
my chest
the earth never really crashes down
it is just blood
pooling at my feet

Rose Red And

Meandering thoughts
A brave, little hart timid
betrayed by the frost

See the hiding of the sunlight?

He finds it hard to see the shadows,
consumed by spaces between

our bodies our

skin and what we know

     our time lost in

 a brittle embraces

The sun shudders
cold burning and I know
He want to leave but I crave
 the sin.

     And outside

braces wintertime
melancholy huntsman prowls
faithful to the bone.

ANON

Passing sentiment, however hard it tries,
Will always be holy
if only for its fragility

Like a heartless cruelty, poets would like us to believe.
the hearts proper placement
bloody on our sleeves we

       allow this sense we
       recognize its convenience

even when we burn with longing
a second's glance will always be holy
for all the lives we give to dreaming

each love a new creation
fragile
cruel but always in its proper
placement.

How High The Roof Beam?

solid somehow
means safety
comfort
and you always listen
eyes bright lips
bowed in secret humor
you created me from
spaces reaching for
roots
a comfortable weight
to wrap yourself in

and you know

my tendency to bluff and brazen
barbwire wrapped 'round
my tissue paper heart and you

know why I have to pretend
I don't see them
pointing fingers with whispering hands

and you somehow know
my exact dimensions
curving yourself around me
palms flat to support me
you gave me
skylines
cityscapes
country sides

a comfortable weight
pressed against me
 always there to keep me
safe to keep me
sane.

Fable And Custom

lover you must know
we are delicate, oleander drifting
timid and anxious
waiting spreading
warmth and I wonder
if you could almost feel
my body
aching

lover you must know
I am only a collection
rust red petals
racing
thunder
and the smell of your skin

desperate and
waiting

lover you must
know

you are the sweetest
poison my most careful
death.

Not Quite Dawn

The muscles and planes of your body
in silhouette
the city outside is hushed
closed inward
and while you sleep I dedicate
 to you the horizon and
        while you sleep I am
bold draping myself in gold and
copper colors
I gift you
sunlight and shadows
      slanting through
      venetian blinds

I give you poetry casting
glory to the roughhewn callouses
the bottoms of your feet singing holy
hosannas to the lace of your eyelashes
I give you
these quiet moments
your body glowing in bas-relief
and the way you reach out for me
like the sun you gather me
so close
      reminding me I am more than
just your heart's beat reminding me
how much you complete me
the sun blankets us in gilded yellows and rich glowing ambers
      and I tuck myself
closer

curling up within your scent
the city flows onward in distant
thrumming engines and the half-heard babble of street noise
while we sleep.

When Embers Remain

The years could have been kinder maybe my love and
my face once sharp and smooth
netted in wrinkles and my knees hold fire
and I still
remember you as a whirlwind
irresistible
we were so young
and I thought I
     understood why my skin did not seem to be enough to
hold
     you and
I remember you were a tidal wave pulling me
underneath and I could just barely
catch my breath.

Oh, yes the years could have been kinder maybe
I remember every creaking ache
every bone deep bruise and I

still remember

the dryness of my lips...

The Heart Is

Ramshackle pasteboard
floral print
wood grain grooved
black paint
in no imagination a
forest
beige carpet knitted whorls
the scent of
previous ghosts

      laying tread fainter now we are
      so modern we
move on

cast iron

dust collector
banked in smaller dimensions
corner and hinge

taste like me
my youth
rotting barefoot
dancing

in the brilliance your smile illuminates
 a yearning for another habitation I have been
running for years
my frozen concrete heart

I have been running for years
gathering weight and scar tissue
will your smooth my edges?
will your lips be enough
to keep me here

In His Kiss

In the silence you rush inward
      further each year you
tell me
      your stories of scarcity of
breath
    and I watch the way your lips move
so I too somehow become
      complicit in
each broken
Window pane in
Back alleys and the
Random bits and
          Pieces of all the things you would
Have me
Believe in the violence
Of broken streamers and dirty glass.

You have always been
five sticky fingers so wanton
      curiously you only said we only had your life to
live so
selfish you were making faces
in the rearview mirror so
nonchalant you knew I could only follow in my
quiet ways you knew I was
      almost nonexistent
      clutching your tight-fisted
      suffocation while I
      gave you your name with
      blue lips I gave you soft bones

broken breath and my desperation
eventually you will find me again
you said draped in linen and smudged cotton
lips slightly parted
and forgiven.

Tell Me Where My True Love Lies

This I have told you it is
all that I have left and I know
      at least on some level that
my skin is so much thicker now

      the bones of my fingers barely bend
      I have stone packed against my
      joints

and well-worn tracks my body follows

because it has to and I have learned to
pretend it is enough

paper masks and empty smiles
 I will tell you
      I can love you even
when I have no clue
how that feels
      my blunt finger tips barely register
      the seams of your body

tracing what I have been told you have
told me
and I pretend
I almost believe
it.

Lament Of The Iron Mask

No slate grey steel
slashed bars
    my love moves erratically half aborted awkward gestures
bruised elbows unfolding in half-understood intentions I

just wanted you to be mine I just wanted to
be enough

       my love tears hair and skin and I am
       always afraid to let you in

I am sorry I kept my eyes closed
ankle pierced you gave me chains that I
could understand no

sharp grey steel to keep
my love closer and closer
half-understood you try
my bleeding skin
     unfolding
I just wanted you to be
a metal gate bracing
      all the weakness in my skin bruised my love
tears and I am always so afraid
     to let you in

Just Say You Love Me

Coal bright
hotbox beaten thin
heartbox
slick sensuality
your face fragmented
pulling waves

the breadth and width
brow to chin
glow
eyes spark flint

the world will end in
fire

Panegyric

Rest easy he said
the earth is soft with loam
with clay walls to embrace you
and keep you safe.

You will dream of roots
spiraling downward to
connect you. You will
dream of younger days
garlanded in energetic
swaths of green.

The sky will swirl and parade
above you marching to trembling
clouds and the sparkling of stars and

We will remember
bad jokes
and inappropriate laughter and
we will carry the light of your smile
until we meet again and he said

Rest easy my friend embraced
in soft loam and clay in your dreams
of vivid green and bright skies
until the day we will find ourselves
again in each other's arms.

So I Don't have To

dangerously your fingertips tangled delicately in the way my body
bends inside your pleasure
each sound tells a fragile telling and I am
vulnerable trembling
beneath your sliding warmth

      savoring everything I allow myself and you want me to
      in space you want me to believe in my own in rhythm
      perfectly tucked behind battered bars and twists of crimson

 you say you can taste my salt upon your lips caught up in the
language of our bodies language
each breath creates shapes in the air above us we will create
our own gravity trailing fingertips
lips and tongue and we will
tell our own stories of hidden warmth
and magnetism your voice a feather light whisper
and you make me promises I

will never know you say
unless I try.

First Time

Fugitive twilight
tiny, weak aluminum heart
embraces betrayal

The Past Has Passed

Somehow I know this will be the last time
and I know you tried
reminding me how tenuous the connection of time and
space
tonight we will hold our breath with trembling hands we
will clutch sweat slick arms and legs
eyes closed pretending we will remember
shoulders and hips pretending
our silence will be enough

     Tomorrow you will be
     someone else
and
I will build a pyre from every
freeze framed cruelly smiling mask
silly matching sweaters and that barely rescued
crumpled receipt for where that forgettable corner store where
you said I first reeled you in
Oh I know
I was foolish to forget how foolish it is to think
our fleeting bodies would somehow be enough
but you tried to remind me
     eventually there will be other lives and
     other loves and this time too will fade and
become bittersweet

Ode To Trifles And Trinkets

Broken boy you were told
words will eventually feel like
this
 fever pitched
suffocation and yes you will
caress each ridge and bone

       morning bright you
       dig your home
       farming flesh to make you
       whole

Broken boy or so you say
you never felt
all the ways they fit you in

       cupboard love you feed
       your soul
       wrinkled bodies with tissue
       skin

fever pitched
oh yes you will
dig your home
broken hearts and
tattered string
Broken boy you were told
words will eventually
pull you in.

Love; Onto The Very Gates Themselves

       In their bones they
believe they are thunder; casted
iron cages scaffolding
a make
shift
love and they stand with

open hands
       like crimson petals feeling only
       the way the sky
       pulls
each line and hemisphere
bodies surrounded
       by a riot of meadows
       roots
       stems and
trees and

barely
       have their skin
       to keep hedged in
rules, codes, youth, and reign

in their bones they shake and rage
barbed wire teeth
          and rotted veins
          rusted iron
each time has passed and

       dawn finds them buried

under scythe and quill mouths muffled
and forgotten rotten lips sealed
with no more
stories left to tell.

Shape Changer

You made yourself a collection
of objects
angles
needle eyes; small tendrils
squat roots and you expected sunlight to
taste like
warmth and dust

and what you give
ligaments naturally
lead to bones and a need to be
held
worshiped
loved

you gather skin
darting the edges in
your eyes
never could hold
saw dust and gravel roads
wear you down

you wanted
proportions
lined just so
smooth
smooth
skin
with hints of gold
muscles curved
and stacked
just enough to be enough

and dimly you reflected

you became a stranger you
no longer recognize

Counter-fit

It doesn't matter if I wanted you
or if I allowed myself
room to think about of how I could possibly fit
cradled in you

breath will only hold so much

I can see the way he looks at you
and I can feel

the way you move
lips quirked and teeth sharpened
I know

he can taste you
heavy and sweet
irresistible

bodies built
and molded and I can
feel

the smoothing of hair and skin and
your breath slides along his hollows and curves
and you are so warm so
complete...

You are so beautiful.

Proof And Property

This too is a weakness a
fragility made from greeting card greed
       we are bound by the spaces we create
       our bodies become holy
become defined by everything we are told we
need.

And we want this
delicate lies and bright painted pictures or
       maybe we need to know we
       are still happy to be still
       lost and hopeful and
restlessly sleepless.

Of course we know of artifice
scripted call and response
words and poetry
       we tangle each other up
       in veins and heart strings
       wants we are told are needs

And we want this of course we know
we are bound by greeting card greed
scripted we are still happy to be
lost and hopeful
This too is a weakness.

Catch

Spirit falls
the body tells all
the deadweight
attraction
red lips and the
way you taste.

Grit and sand

makes its own gravity

eventually and the

we move so fast

barely taking breath

we try

gnashing teeth

bitten tongue

red lips

and the way you
taste hooked fingers
devouring me like a kiss.

Crust Punks and Travelers

He had
electric coursing
in his veins
the city moved with his
heartbeat
he would flash his
punk rock smile
slim and smooth arms
safety pins

the shells of his hips
cresting above thrift store finds
pale and authentically
hungry he once

tasted of nicotine
intoxicating and
forbidden
and what would
your parents think?

you would trace
the bones of his body
his lips
the way his eyes would burn
so bright
marking scars and streetsigns and
you would always be there
and one day
they would see

you were starving.

Dream Girl

She was the tower
and the lake
whispering trees and
make believe she
saw the world with
blue-grey glass fingers
barely touching the window's
pane.

She was
patchworked dreams
and fine stitching
a clockwork heart
muttering to itself she was
myth and magic and
everything you
wanted to believe

She was the tower
and the lake
cool tides
to pull you under
in your sleep

She was dark currents
and the way you
cannot breathe
something new a
challenging game

She is the tower and
the lake your hearbeat
weighing heavy in your chest
whispering trees and make-believe and
all the things you wanted
her to be.

Just Letting Love In

This is just the tiniest little baby steps...
think about this as safety pins, Vaseline, blood, and
the familiar constriction of living in the past.

Today, I had an image of myself as just phantom carrying
a corroded lead plated heart
moving from room to room ah, my usual haunts.

Today, I opened the door and looked down
concrete steps and a delicate metal railing.
down there the music is blaring and incoherent
and they speak so loudly on their status symbol
speaker-phones

think about this as just the ramblings
of a passing phantom.
think about this as another cliché
without an accent mark.

Today, I made tough decisions and
then promptly, pulled the covers up over my head.
Today, I did my best but I have yet
to cross the threshold.

Oh! Icarus I have loved you

Each year digs a little deeper and every second,
I realize that i am sinking and yet
somedays, I believe i can remember you moving like clouds beneath
me
somedays, I believe I can remember
the movement of your calloused palms caressing me
like an ocean of light warm against my skin
and you lifted me so high I could only gasp for air but
broken wings can only hold so much and each year
demands a little more
digging deeper and every second I realize
      I am losing you
      one tattered useless memory
      at a time.

I Needed This

He was made from lifelines
heart lines
open arms spanning the horizon

delicate he was
every 3pm movement
outside he

was made from distances
the culmination of illicit substances
finely textured

He was made from scar tissue
years cutting at soft tissue
broad shoulders casually
mesmerizing he

was made from missed chances
and every 3pm lonely
lunch time

an apparition he was
delicate tissues
scarred heart lines
reaching desperately
outside

My Phantom

I don't want more than
what I can hold with
my eyes closed
        I don't want him
        to be all the things I
        can't control
                I am so thin now I am
                see through and all I have
                left is the accumulation of
                fat and flesh
                I don't want more
                of what I cannot be
                and all the things I
                think he needs
        I am so empty now I am
        past through and all I was given
        is everything he thinks he
        needs
I don't want more than
what I can hold I
don't want him to
want me
anymore.

Prisoner

Fixed
in this moment
you will always
be leaving
me to
follow your
footsteps
trying to hold
onto
the scent of
your body
over me
pulling
down and
through
and
eventually
I will
release you

Love's Story

And it has been told
carved out like
a windowless heart
less smoke than ash and
hollow listening walls
he wanted more

And it is been said that
the years took
first marrow then
bone and
learned men

narrowed eyes like microscopes
looking to find
him wandering thoughts and
desperation
carving the walls to
watch Him bleed and He knows

I spent all those years
looking for a vein

party boy. Plays well with others
and His story was read in torn plastic crumbled
into threadbare carpets in the backs
of cars
he led him forward promises less than
lullabies more like an ache
for an open door
at another inevitable porch light ending

first the marrow; then the bone

And I told him I loved graveyards
holding dust in my heart like stone
widowless with broken glass
just another

familiar steel trap well used and
pretentious and
I can still feel
eventually.

he pulls his strings teasing he named him
party boy familiar stories they say are
told in pools of crimson and
carmine
dried out and stained teeth like
rust.

Eventually there are no promises
no safety net strung
from the distant glow from porch light and open doors.

And learned men with narrow eyes
look for clues and
personal growth
carved into crumbling walls

finger prints smudging thinner skin
but we all know
our greedy ghost live in the bends and
folds pressed into
torn plastic packages wasted
and we
know we have wasted too many years
looking first the marrow
then the bone.

Drawing Near

Spring fades and skin
thickens; collects bruises; scars
another year lost to love.

Made in the USA
San Bernardino, CA
30 December 2017